R ROBOT
Saves Lunch

by R. Nicholas Kuszyk

G. P. Putnam's Sons

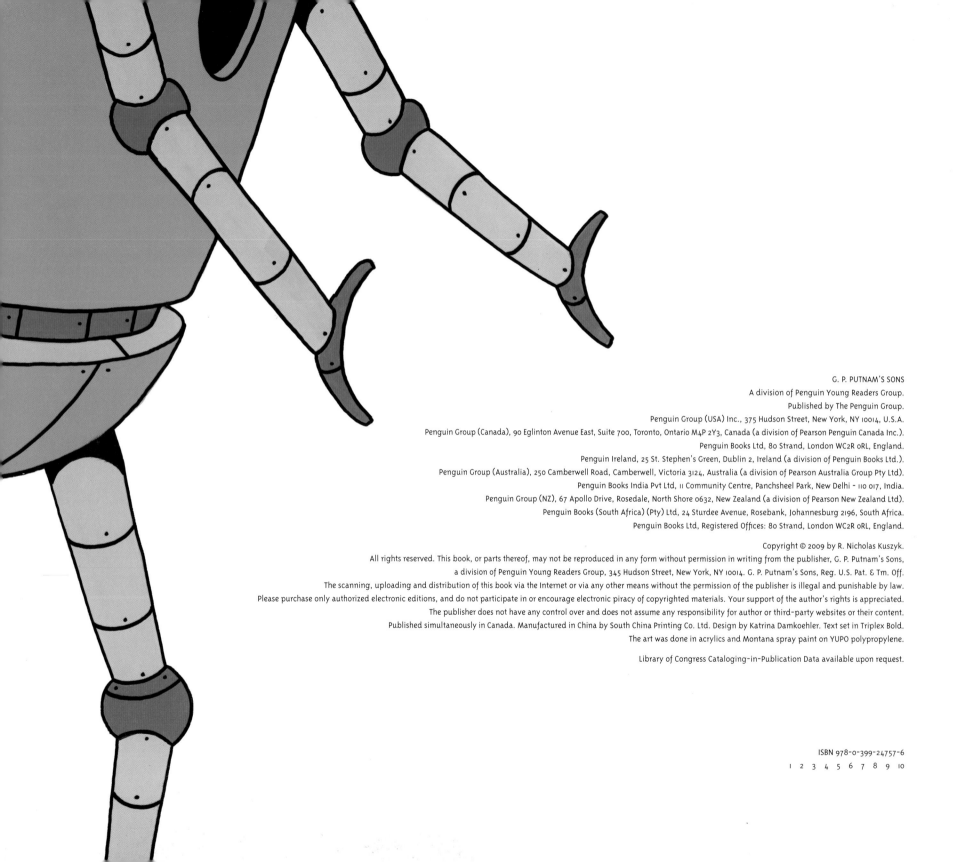

G. P. PUTNAM'S SONS

A division of Penguin Young Readers Group.

Published by The Penguin Group.

Penguin Group (USA) Inc., 375 Hudson Street, New York, NY 10014, U.S.A.

Penguin Group (Canada), 90 Eglinton Avenue East, Suite 700, Toronto, Ontario M4P 2Y3, Canada (a division of Pearson Penguin Canada Inc.).

Penguin Books Ltd, 80 Strand, London WC2R 0RL, England.

Penguin Ireland, 25 St. Stephen's Green, Dublin 2, Ireland (a division of Penguin Books Ltd.).

Penguin Group (Australia), 250 Camberwell Road, Camberwell, Victoria 3124, Australia (a division of Pearson Australia Group Pty Ltd).

Penguin Books India Pvt Ltd, 11 Community Centre, Panchsheel Park, New Delhi - 110 017, India.

Penguin Group (NZ), 67 Apollo Drive, Rosedale, North Shore 0632, New Zealand (a division of Pearson New Zealand Ltd).

Penguin Books (South Africa) (Pty) Ltd, 24 Sturdee Avenue, Rosebank, Johannesburg 2196, South Africa.

Penguin Books Ltd, Registered Offices: 80 Strand, London WC2R 0RL, England.

Published simultaneously in Canada. Manufactured in China by South China Printing Co. Ltd. Design by Katrina Damkoehler. Text set in Triplex Bold.

The art was done in acrylics and Montana spray paint on YUPO polypropylene.

Library of Congress Cataloging-in-Publication Data available upon request.

ISBN 978-0-399-24757-6

1 2 3 4 5 6 7 8 9 10

Dedicated to
my
father

and my

    mother

and my

    sister Jenny,

       and Dennis

and nephew Nicholas too

      of course.

R Robot has to hurry to get to the robot factory. So he brushes his teeth, takes a shower, eats breakfast, puts on his shoes, and walks his dog—all at the same time!

He always brings an extra head to work, just in case.

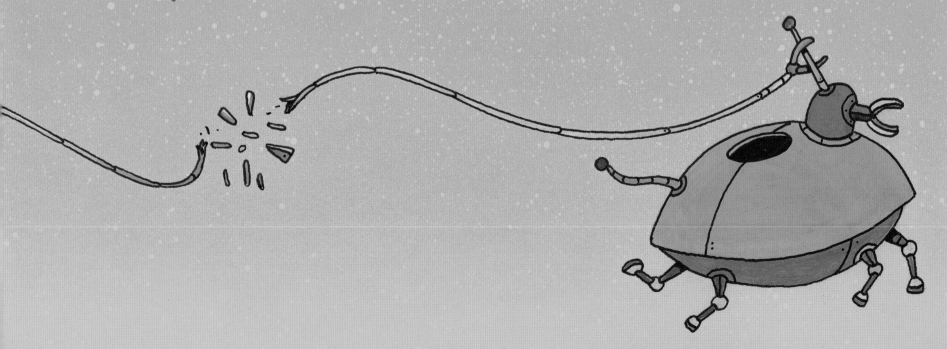

The bus is so crowded,
he has to ride
to the robot factory
on the roof!

R Robot's job today is to help his friends find the missing robot who was last seen at lunchtime the day before.

They took under the heavy tubs.

They reach up
in
high places.

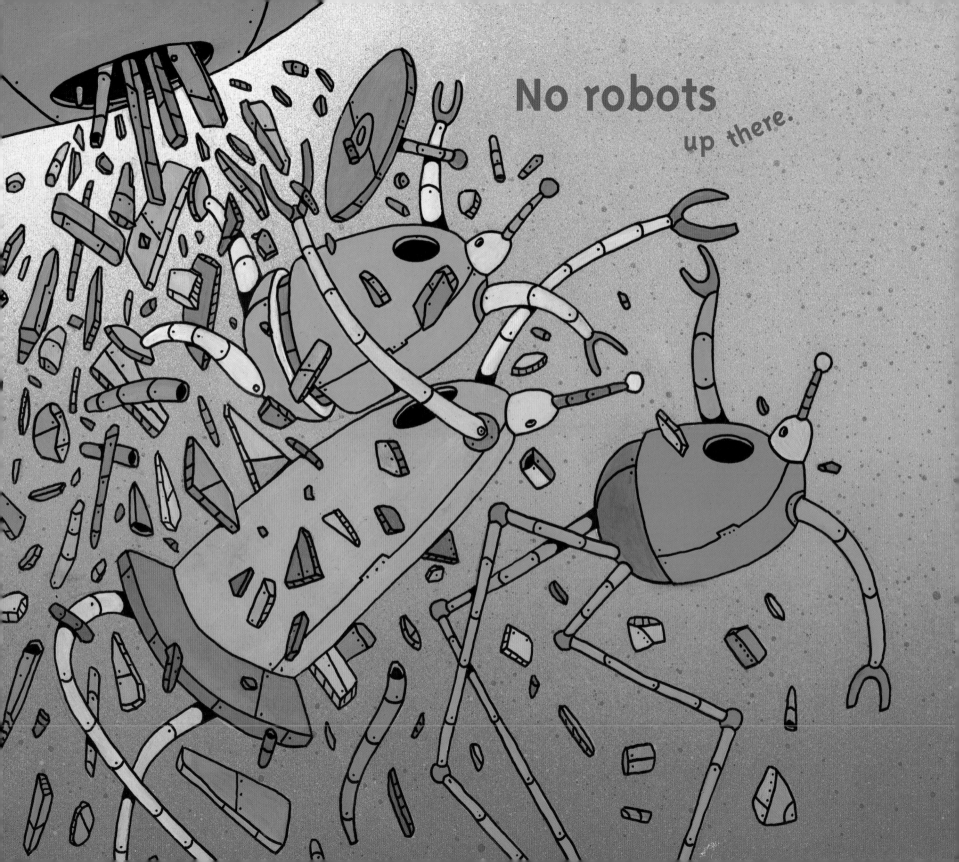

But they clean it all up before lunchtime.

The lunch line is super long because the Big Cooker robot is clogged

and no one knows how to fix him.

His friends lower R Robot into **Big Cooker's belly.**

Big Cooker's belly is dark and scary,
until R Robot turns on the flashlight
on his extra head.

R Robot almost gets stuck in the mess as he searches for the problem.

Outside Big Cooker, the robots are
hungry and worried about R Robot.

Out shoots R Robot and the missing robot.
The clog is fixed!

Because R Robot saved lunch . . . .

. . . and the
missing
robot too
of course.

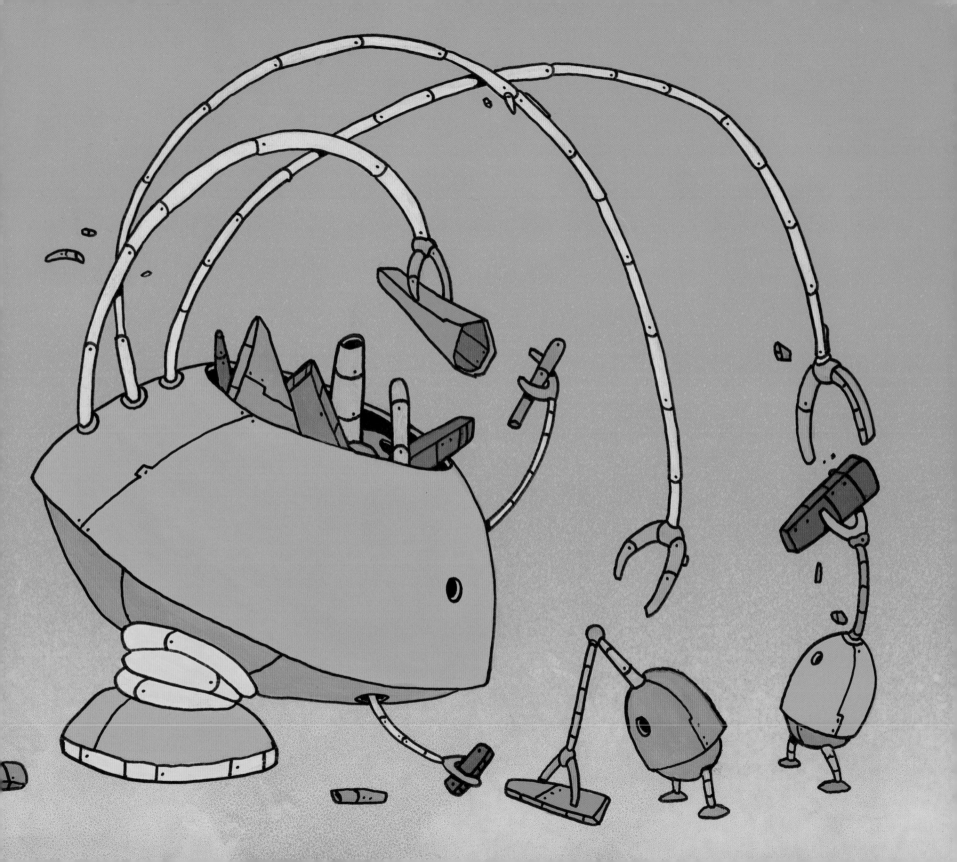

The End

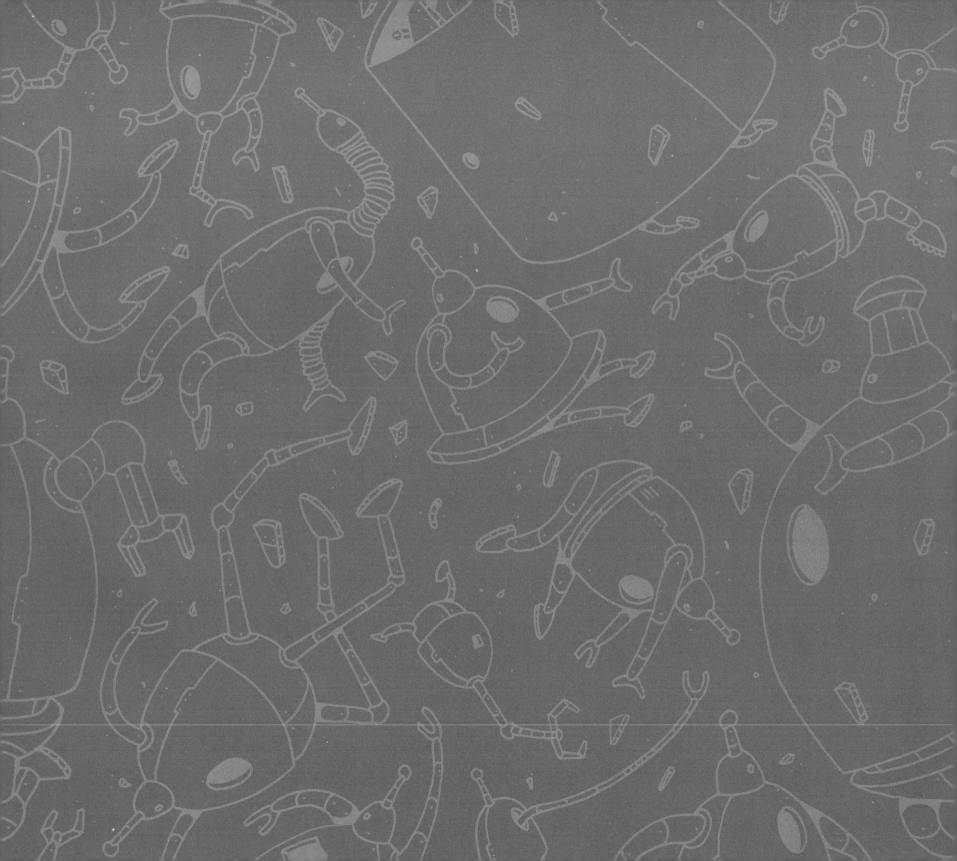